SAVING HADLEY

AMY SPARLING

ONE

The hallways of Shady Lane High are filled with the happy sounds of students on the last day of school. And yet I'm stuck in the counselor's office. With only fifteen minutes left until the final bell rings for the day, sending us all out into our summer break, the last thing I expected was a note from the office requesting my presence in Mrs. Smith's office. But I guess I know why I'm here, and I shouldn't be surprised.

The counselor in question walks into her office after I've been sitting in here for five minutes. She doesn't seem to be in any hurry even though school is almost out. She smells like coffee and strawberry vape juice and she offers me a tight-lipped smile as she sits at her desk.

"Hello, Hadley."

"Hi." My voice is too meek and I wish I'd sat a little

straighter and spoken a little...smarter? Maybe then she'd have mercy on me.

Mrs. Smith laces her fingers together on top of her desk. She sat like this the last two times I was called down to her office. I can't tell if she thinks it's a friendly pose or an intimidating one. Her lips dip into a frown. "Do you know why you're here?"

I gnaw on the inside of my lip. "My chemistry final?"

Maybe if my chemistry teacher hadn't taken so long to upload the test grades online, I could have seen this meeting coming. But alas, I have no idea what grade I got on this ill-fated test of the sciences. It's the one subject that I've never seemed to grasp like everyone else does. Algebra? History? Pre-cal? Piece of cake. But chemistry is this elusive mash of numbers and letters and terminology I just can't stand.

Mrs. Smith nods. "I'm afraid so. You received a sixty-seven on your final exam yesterday."

My chest falls. Sixty-seven. That's just three points below what I needed to barely scrape by this year with a C average and pass the class.

"I tried," I say, but the look on her face tells me it's futile to beg for mercy now. She warned me a month ago that if I didn't get my grades up, I'd fail and have to take summer school. "I really did try. I don't know why I suck so much."

Her severe expression softens just a tad. "You don't suck, Hadley. You are a valuable student and you have all the potential in the world. However..." She lets out a sigh as she flips through some paperwork on her desk. "You will need to attend summer school. I've already spoken with your parents and they've agreed to online schooling."

I wince when she says *parents*. Plural. I don't have parents, not in the way she's saying. I have my dad and then the stepmom, Lucy. She's not related to me. She doesn't raise me, she doesn't take care of me. The most she's ever done was toss me a box of tissues that time I had the flu and tell me to go to my room so I don't make anyone else sick. Lucy absolutely does not deserve the title of parent. After my short internal rant about the woman who lives in my house, I realize what Mrs. Smith just said.

"Online schooling?"

"Yes, dear. You won't have to come up here for summer school. You can take the online chemistry course from home. It's a three week intensive course but I know you'll do well. I believe in you."

"Well, I guess that's not so bad." Nothing screams *loser* quite like showing up to school when everyone else is on their summer break.

She nods. "And you'll get to start your senior year on time with no problems. I look forward to you graduating next year with all A's."

"Don't get your hopes up," I say with a snort.

She grins. "I believe in you, kiddo." She slides some papers under the automatic stapler on her desk which binds them in the corner with a *thunk*. "Here's your paperwork. The course is given through the local community college. That's your username and password. You have all summer to get it done, but I suggest starting early. That way you're not scrambling at the last minute."

"Thanks," I say, taking the papers. I stand up and sling my backpack over my shoulder, feeling about two feet tall. What kind of seventeen-year-old can't even pass basic chemistry? I am a loser of the largest degree. Ugh.

I spend the last few minutes before the bell rings standing in the hallway trying not to cry. I knew this was a possibility. I've heard my dad and stepmom berate me for the last month about it, ever since Mrs. Smith sent a letter home saying I was in danger of failing. I really did try to pass this final exam, not that it matters. All those hours of studying while my boyfriend edited his YouTube videos beside me were all for nothing. I still failed. I could have been having fun with my friends instead of studying chemical equations.

I take a deep breath and will the tears away. Lane will be here any second and he'll make everything better. We've only been dating for three months, but he's totally the best. Extremely cute and even more popular. I've kind of had a crush on him ever since junior high when I was a dorky thirteen-year-old with braces and he was on the football team. He didn't even know who I was back then, but then it all changed during spring break when I saw him at a party. Our eyes met from across Blake Asher's swimming pool, and he smiled at me. We exchanged numbers and spent the whole night hanging out. Three days later, he was my official boyfriend.

The final bell rings. I smile at the happy memories and scan the crowd of students until I find Lane. He's easy to spot because he's the only person holding out a selfie stick while he walks through the throngs of people in the main hallway. Lane's YouTube channel—The Right Lane— is something of a legend here at Shady Lane High. He finally got a hundred thousand subscribers a few months ago and things have really taken off since then. He must be documenting the last day of his senior year. He's officially free from high school today. I, however, am stuck for another year.

"Lane!" I call out, waving to him. He sees me and cuts across the hallway, talking to this phone while he walks. I can't hear what he's saying, but it's probably something like *here's my girlfriend, let's go say hi to her*. Over the last three months of us dating, his YouTube channel has gotten to know me as well as Lane knows me.

I reach out to hug him because I could really use a hug right now, but his arm wraps around my shoulders and kind of guides me out of the way. Maybe he wants some privacy, but I'm not sure why because he's still holding out that stupid selfie stick recording us. There is no privacy when the world is watching.

"I just had the stupidest meeting ever," I say as he walks us down a quiet hallway near the art classrooms.

"Listen, Hadley," Lane says, leaning his back against the wall. He shifts his selfie stick until both of our faces are in the frame. I see words scrolling across the screen and I realize he's on YouTube live. He's not recording a video to edit and post later—he's streaming it live to his fans right now.

"What's up?" I say, feeling more than awkward since I'm on the video. It's not the first time I've been featured on his videos—we've even done several "Ask my Girlfriend Q&A" videos, but they've always been pre-recorded so he can edit out the parts where I mess up.

"As you know, it's my last day of school." He looks me in the eye, so it's easy to think we're having this conversation alone, but we're not. His phone is still facing us as he holds it out, keeping us in frame.

"Yeah?" I say, wishing whatever he's doing will hurry up and be over so I can tell him about my summer school situation without the camera rolling.

"And I'm going to college in the fall."

"I know."

He stares at me for a long moment, and I almost wonder if he asked me some question and he's waiting on an answer. Then he reaches up with his free hand

and cups my cheek. "I can't start off college with a girl-friend. I'm sure you understand."

My throat goes dry. "Wait... what?"

"We're done, babe." Lane turns to the phone camera and winks at it. He freaking *winks* at it! "We had our fun but... this is a breakup video."

Tears flood my eyes. It's too hard to hold them back because I've been on the verge of crying ever since I was called to the counselor's office. They aren't small quiet tears either. I'm full on crying like a total idiot. Lane pats my shoulder all while keeping the camera focused on me.

"You'll be all right," he says, but there's nothing consoling or friendly in his voice. He's become the YouTube personality that everyone loves. A cocky, handsome jerk.

I'm not much for swearing, but I swear now. I tell him exactly what he can do with his stupid YouTube videos. I hate the look of satisfaction he gets at my reaction. Drama is great for viewers, after all. I turn and run down the hallway, not stopping until I'm on the sidewalk and off school property. My tears blur my vision, but I've walked home from school every day for three years, so I know where I'm going even if the sidewalk beneath my feet is out of focus.

The sun is shining here in Texas, and by all standards, it's a beautiful summer day. But I can't enjoy it. My chest is heaving from running and crying and my face is soaked. My eyes hurt. My heart hurts. Everything hurts. I walk a couple more blocks, wishing I lived closer than two miles away from the school.

As if this day couldn't get any worse, my head starts to ache in that familiar and haunting way that tells me a migraine is coming. Great. Just great. Once a migraine hits me, I'm out for the count. They're absolutely brutal, they happen about twice a year, and apparently they're genetic. My mom gets them too, according to my dad. I wouldn't know because ever since she divorced my dad, married someone new, and moved away when I was a toddler, I haven't seen her.

I'm still a mile away from home, and pain explodes through my head. There's no way I can make it home right now. Luckily, I'm only a few houses away from my cousin Destiny, who is also my best friend. We're the same age, but she's homeschooled now after getting in a little too much trouble over the years. My aunt and uncle got sick of her sneaking out to parties and getting high on campus, so they yanked her out of school last year. I'm pretty sure we wouldn't be friends if we weren't related because I am not into anything like that. Still, she's always there when I need her. I text her and see if she's home, and she's happy to have me to come over and ride out the migraine.

Then I call my dad and tell him what's going on.

"Is this a real migraine or are you trying to avoid talking about how you failed chemistry?" The tone of Dad's voice tells me he thinks it's the latter.

My teeth clench together from the pain. "Dad, I'm seriously dying here. I need to go lay down."

"Okay," he says and I can practically see his frown through the phone. "But if I find out you're lying, you'll be even more grounded than you are now. I'm working late tonight, but I'll pick you up later."

My cousin is rocking a pair of pink fuzzy pajamas when she opens the door. "Hey!" she says, all smiles. "It's good to see you."

I hung out with Destiny a lot more before I started dating Lane, but now I can't remember the last time I came over. We text a lot but haven't hung out much lately. I've been a both crappy cousin *and* student, it seems.

"Where's Aunt Emma?" I ask, pressing my hands against my forehead. Destiny's mom works from home and she's usually the one who answers the door.

"My parents are away for the weekend. Some B&B up in Denton." She rolls her eyes. "They're trying to keep the romance alive."

"Romance is stupid," I mutter. "I'm gonna go lay down." They have the best guest bedroom ever, complete with blackout curtains and a fluffy comfortable mattress.

"Okay." She closes the front door behind me. "I'm having a few friends over later, but we're just going to watch a movie, so we'll be quiet. If you start feeling better you should join us."

"I doubt it," I say as I make my way down the hallway to the guest room. "But thanks for the offer."

In the quiet room, I drop my backpack to the floor, then realize the soft buzzing sound is coming from my phone, not my ears. I retrieve it from the zippered pocket on my backpack and turn the screen brightness down as low as it gets. My migraine is in full force right now and everything makes it hurt worse.

There are thirty two new messages on my phone and a few missed calls from my friends.

It looks like Lane's breakup video has gone viral.

Great. Just great.

TWO

"Hadley."

My head is pounding. My thoughts are foggy. Everything is... flashing red and blue? It takes me a second to realize I'm waking up. It takes me even longer to realize I'm not in my own bed. My eyes open, and I blink a few times. The walls are flashing red and blue from something in the window. My head pounds, but at least it's not as bad as it was earlier.

"Hadley. Wake up this second!"

My stepmom Lucy's voice shatters the last bits of sleep from my brain. I sit up, my head throbbing with the movement. "What's going on?" I ask groggily.

"What's *going on*, is that you've been caught," she snaps.

"Huh?"

I look up and see Lucy standing in front of me in Destiny's guest bedroom, her hands on her hips and that scowl of hers etched on her face. It's dark outside, save for the red and blue lights that I now realize are coming from a cop car. My heart pounds. "Is everyone okay? What happened?"

"I think you know exactly what happened," my dad says as he enters the room. He's still wearing his khaki pants and dry-cleaned work shirt which means he probably hasn't been home yet.

"Actually, I don't know," I say, running my hands through my hair. Beside me, my phone is blinking and lighting up with new messages.

Lucy sees me look at it and she snatches it up. "Say goodbye to your phone."

"What, why?"

"Get up," Dad snaps. "We'll go over your punishment in the car. Thank God the cops aren't going to arrest you."

"I figured it was just a matter of time before I got a call from the police about her," Lucy says under her breath. I scowl. I'm a good person. I have no reason to get in trouble with the cops.

In the living room, my cousin is looking extremely guilty while an officer talks to her. Half empty bottles of liquor and beer are on the coffee table, and there's even an ash tray and the scent of marijuana in the air. In some states, that's legal, but in Texas it is definitely not.

I give Destiny a WTF look as I walk past her, my dad and stepmom flanking me. She shrugs in this way that I guess is supposed to be apologetic. But she just looks annoyed, not sorry.

A few teenagers I've never seen before are standing in the front yard, their hands cuffed behind their back.

"I am so disappointed in you," Dad says as he opens the backdoor of his car and waits for me to climb inside.

"Wish I could say I was surprised," Lucy chimes in.

Dad waves at the cops and then we drive home. The short mile home takes no time at all, and soon me and my aching head are standing in our living room while my dad and stepmom glare at me.

"Care to explain yourself?" Dad says. His nostrils flare. He's never been this mad at me before. Of course, I've never really been in trouble before, either.

"There's nothing to explain..." I wince and grip my forehead. "Can I just go to bed? My head is killing me."

"I'm sure it is," Dad says angrily. "That's what drugs and alcohol will do to you. You think you hurt now? It'll be worse in the morning."

"Dad, I didn't do anything," I say, wishing my head didn't hurt so bad so I could put more conviction in my voice. "I swear. I got a migraine and just went to Destiny's house and fell asleep."

Lucy barks out a laugh. "How stupid do you think we are?"

"You can smell my breath if you want." I shrug. "It

won't smell like alcohol. You can drug test me. I promise I didn't do anything."

"First you failed chemistry, and now this." I guess my dad is just going to ignore my pleas for a drug test. And while I'm thinking about it, how messed up is it that I'm begging for a drug test to prove my innocence? My dad should trust me more than this.

"Just because your boyfriend dumped you doesn't mean you can go off and get wasted," Lucy says. Each word pierces through my heart.

"How did you know about that?" I ask. The pain of this migraine almost made me forget about Lane's humiliating video. Now my whole body floods with the heat of embarrassment at knowing my stepmom most definitely watched me get dumped online.

Lucy rolls her eyes. "Everyone knows about it."

"You went viral." The soft voice in the corner comes from my stepsister Kyndall. I didn't even realize she was in the room until she spoke. I look over at her and she gives me a sad smile. "I'm sorry, Hadley. That really sucks."

"You should be more like your sister," Dad says. I cringe. Just like Lucy isn't my parent, Kyndall isn't my sister. Sure we live in the same house, but we are not even remotely close. She's the uber-smart student with an overachieving high school itinerary. I'm a regular student with a regular, boring life.

"I agree," Lucy says, flashing a loving smile to her daughter. "This year Kyndall got into Harvard and you flunked school and started drinking. For two girls who grew up together, I wish you could be more alike."

"I didn't drink!" I yell it even though it makes my head hurt worse. "I didn't do anything! I just took a nap. Why won't you believe me?"

Dad frowns and heaves a sigh. "You need a change of scenery, Hadley. You're going down the same path as Density... drugs... drinking... partying... I'm putting a stop to it now."

He looks over at my stepmom who nods at him. I get the feeling they've already talked about this before. Dad turns to me. "Go to bed. In the morning, you'll pack up enough clothes for the summer. You're going to stay with Grandad."

"What?" Maybe my headache is making me hallucinate things. My only living grandparent is a grumpy old man in Virginia who I've seen every other Christmas while I was growing up, since my dad and Lucy alternate which family we visit for the holidays. "I don't even know Grandad."

"Now's the perfect time to get to know him," Dad says. "I think the change of scenery will be good for you."

WHEN I WAKE up in the morning, my migraine is finally gone but my situation in life is still just as bleak as ever. I'd tried to beg my dad over breakfast to let me stay home this summer, but he didn't budge. Apparently, my Grandad is looking forward to my visit, but I'm not sure I believe that. The man and I have hardly spoken any words to each other besides hello and goodbye. He's not exactly mean, but he's not friendly.

I cry the whole time I pack up my suitcase. The heartbreak of Lane has settled in, and I'm not sure if I'm sad that we're over, or sad that he filmed it, or both. What a jerk. I hate him so much, but ripping up the photo of him that's on my wall doesn't make me feel any better. Dad finally gives me my phone back since I'll need it in Virginia, and I have so many notifications I don't even want to read them all.

Most of the messages are my friends freaking out about the YouTube video and offering their condolences. One message is from Destiny, sent this morning.

So sorry about last night! I didn't think the party would get that crazy and I'm sorry you got in trouble too! Love you!

I roll my eyes and decide not to reply back to her just yet. I love her because she's my cousin and friend, but her stupid party really ruined my life. Of course Lane ruined it first, and he hasn't messaged me at all. I'm starting to wonder if he dated me just to break up with me online. Did he even really like me? Or was I just some stupid game to get more subscribers and likes?

I wipe my tears away and keep my face stone cold

while Dad drives me to the airport. I am all out of begging and pleading. There's nothing left to say. My own dad won't believe me when I tell him I didn't do it. What else can I do but sit here and wallow in misery?

Before long, my plane lands and I use Dad's credit card to order an Uber driver to take me to Grandad's house. The good news is that I haven't cried since we left the house. The bad news is that all I want to do is burst into tears. Luckily, I hold them off for now.

"Welcome to Virginia!" my Uber driver says when I get in his car. He's probably in his mid-twenties and is covered in colorful tattoos. "You here for business or pleasure?"

"I'm here for punishment."

"Ah... okay." He flashes me an uneasy smile in the rear-view mirror. The rest of the drive is silent.

Sterling Beach, Virginia is a sleepy little tourist town on the east coast. Unlike our muddy brown beaches on the coast of Texas, Sterling Beach has bright white sand and beautiful water. I stare out the window as we drive past miles of beach houses. The Welcome to Sterling Beach sign said the population was five thousand, which is about a fifth of the population of my hometown. If your boyfriend broke up with you here, you wouldn't have to be as embarrassed because fewer people would find out about it.

I huff sarcastically to myself. Maybe making jokes about this breakup will be better than crying about it. But it still hurts. It's been twenty-four hours since my boyfriend dumped me like so much useless garbage. On live freaking YouTube, no less.

I close my eyes. *I will not cry.*

My Uber slows down and turns onto a dusty single lane road that leads straight to the beach. We drive past rows and rows of beach houses, heading straight to the water where my Grandad's house has a coveted location right on the beach.

Every time we visit, Dad tries to convince Grandad to sell his home and reap the huge profits that are to be made since the area is getting more popular every year. He doesn't live in the wealthy part of town where large mansions overlook the beach, but he could still make a pretty big profit if he sold his house, especially since his original mortgage has been paid off for decades.

Grandad has lived in this beach house since my dad was a little kid. He always shakes his head, says he got married in this house and will die in this house, and that's the end of the conversation.

We pull up to the house, and like always, not much has changed. The pale blue exterior could use a new coat of paint. So could the whitewashed porch that extends all around the small three-bedroom home. The sound of the ocean is accented by the windchimes that hang from the porch, dancing in the breeze. Grandad's old Chevy truck is parked under the house on the concrete slab. All the beach houses are up on stilts, just in case it ever floods.

I get out and take my suitcase from the trunk.

Grandad must have been watching for me because he walks down the staircase, meeting me at the bottom.

"Hello, Hadley," he says, offering me a small smile. My Grandad is a tall man in his seventies with tanned skin and solid white hair. Marine tattoos line his arms in a reminder of his younger years in the special forces. From the few stories I've heard, my Grandad was a total badass when he was in the military. A force to be reckoned with.

He might be old and wrinkled now, but he's still just as scary to me.

"How was your trip?"

I swallow. "It was fine. Thanks."

His wrinkled expression turns to a smile. "Let me show you to your room."

THREE

I NEVER KNEW MY GRANDMOTHER SINCE SHE DIED before I was born, but I get the feeling that Grandad didn't change much about the house after she passed. There's an antique beach theme going on, with jars filled with shells and nautical décor everywhere. They have white wicker furniture on the porch and in the kitchen dining area. It's easy to imagine a sweet, loving grandma walking out from the kitchen and giving you a grandmotherly smile, just like in the movies. It's too bad she's gone. Maybe Grandad wouldn't be so scary if his wife was here to make him smile more.

I'm staying in my dad's childhood bedroom. Even over the handful of times I've been here for holidays, it was always just a quick visit. Dinner, some socializing, and then back to the hotel or airport to head back home. I don't think I've ever seen inside the bedroom at the end of the hallway until now. My dad was totally a cool surfer dude back in the nineties. His old surf posters are still taped to the wall, dusty and yellowing. His bright red surfboard stands tall in the corner. It's all scuffed up and worn which tells me it wasn't just a decoration. I bet my mom loved that he was a surfer guy. So much has changed since my dad grew up. He's not the least bit laid back or fun now.

The room has two French doors that open onto a small balcony. A small table and chairs are out there, even though you can only barely see the beach from this side of the house because there's another house next door which takes up most of the view. Still, a room with a balcony is pretty cool. I try to open the door, but give up after a few minutes. I guess this room hasn't been used in so long that the doors are stuck.

After two days, I settle into a bit of a routine with Grandad. He wakes up earlier than anyone should ever wake up—like six in the morning—and takes a long walk on the beach. Then he comes back home and makes coffee and breakfast. I really want to stay in bed, sleeping as late as possible, but I also don't feel comfortable helping myself to food in his kitchen, so I go out there and eat whenever he's eating.

Grandad is an amazing cook. He's also a lot different from my own dad. Scary and old, yes, but there are some good qualities here too. Whenever we eat together at my house, my dad likes to sit next to Lucy and pull some of his "united front" crap where they both lecture me on whatever it is that I'm not doing right. Usually, it's something Lucy doesn't like and my dad will just side with her because she's his wife.

My dad is also a big talker. He will talk and talk and talk until I've forgotten what we started talking about in the first place. He doesn't talk about fun stuff, either. It's always, *always*, a lecture. My grades suck. My study habits suck. My friends suck. I should apply myself. I should work harder. I should figure out my college plans even though I still have a whole year left of high school next year.

Blah, blah, blah.

Grandad doesn't do any of that. He tells me good morning when I walk into the kitchen and then hands me a plate and a coffee cup. I fill up my plate with some of everything he's cooked—bacon, eggs, toast and jam are the usual offerings.

And then we eat in silence.

As much as I don't want to be here this summer, I enjoy the silence. It's nice not being constantly told how much you suck. It's also nice being out of my house and away from all the stupid Harvard talk. I don't even know how Kyndall did it. There's nothing special about her besides excellent grades. When we were in fourth grade, I didn't think it was possible to have a 100% average in a class on your report card. Kyndall had five of them. And then in English class, her average was 101 since she always got the extra credit spelling questions correct.

Ugh.

I swallow hard and wish the pain in my chest would go away. Every time I think of Kyndall and how annoying it is to be compared to her, I'll also start to think about Lane and how he ripped my heart out. Then I'll think about my grades. Destiny's party that got me in trouble. Everything that makes me sad will come rising up in my thoughts as if by magic. I don't want to think about any of it, but I can't help it. My brain likes to torture me.

While it's nice to be free from my dad's constant lectures, I'm still here alone, surrounded by the silence. After breakfast, I always go back to my room and work on my summer school assignments until I smell Grandad cooking lunch when I emerge again for another meal. I do the same thing for dinner. It's a good plan. I figure I can spend the whole summer like this—eating Grandad's cooking and then sitting in my dad's old bedroom thinking about everything that's gone wrong with my life.

I keep my phone charged, but after a few days I stop looking at it. The only notifications I get are about that stupid viral video. I can't bring myself to watch it, because who wants to replay their breakup on YouTube? And every one of my so-called friends who dares to text me about it does not get a reply. They don't deserve a reply.

Maybe I'll just sit here in dad's old room forever and never talk to anyone ever again.

About a week goes by—I'm not sure how long because the days are blending together and I'm not counting them—and there's knock on my bedroom door about an hour after dinner.

Deep down I hope it's my dad coming to take me home but I know that's just wishful thinking.

"Come in," I call out.

Grandad slowly opens my door. He's wearing jeans and a black and red plaid shirt. He seems more put together than usual. I give him a small smile while he stands in the doorway.

"How you feeling?" he asks, his voice gruff and to the point.

"Fine."

His dark eyes study me. "You're not sick or anything?"

I shrug. "No." *Not sick. Just heartbroken.*

He nods once. "I've let you mope around in your room all week, but I think it's time we lay down some ground rules."

I stiffen. I guess I knew this was too good to be true. Of course he has rules. This is punishment, after all. Not a vacation. "Okay." My voice is meek and pathetic.

"Your dad says you have school work to do?"

"Yes sir," I say, nodding toward my laptop at the foot of the bed. "I've been working on it every day."

He nods again. "Good. So here's the deal. You can sit in here and hate the world six days a week. But on

Friday, you have to come out of this room. You will join us for Friday night poker."

"I don't really know how to play poker," I admit.

"You don't have to play if you don't want to, but you will join us every Friday night at seven." He takes a step back into the hallway and checks his watch. "That's in ten minutes. Meet us outside."

I don't know what he means by "us" but he walks away before I can ask for clarification. Also, that's not at all how I thought this talk would go. His only rule is for me to hang out at poker night once a week? Despite being related, my dad and grandfather are totally different people.

I'm wearing black spandex workout pants and an old T-shirt I plan on sleeping in. It's from my freshman year when Destiny and I thought it would be fun to run a half marathon. Spoiler alert – it was not fun. All I got from it was blistered feet, a sunburn, and this boring oversized T-shirt. But I guess it's a good enough outfit for sitting outside and watching old people play poker, so I drag myself outside of my room.

The beach house's wraparound porch is twice as wide on the front of the house so there's lots of room to sit out here and watch the beach. In addition to the wicker furniture that's always out here, my Grandad has set up a fold out poker table. It's the kind with cupholders and green felt on top. My Grandad sits at the table along with two old men and one old woman. The three old men are busy talking about property taxes, but the woman sees me the moment I step out on the porch.

"Well hello there," she says warmly as a wrinkled smile lights up her face. She's really tan, with light blue eyes and long white hair that's pulled into a high bun. As far as being old goes, she's not that old. Maybe in her late sixties? She pulls out the folding chair next to her and pats it. "You are very beautiful for being related to this cranky old man."

I chuckle and realize it's the first time I've so much as smiled in a week. "I'm Hadley," I say, sitting next to her.

"I'm Jan. I live three houses to the east," she says with a nod of her head toward that direction. She winks at me. "And I always take old Clint for all he's worth."

"I'm gonna get my ten dollars back," Grandad says, stopping mid conversation to glare at her. "Every dollar of it and then some."

Jan waves away his words with her hand. "Keep talking, old man. You all know I'm the best poker player."

Grandad smiles at her. "It was all luck."

Jan shrugs. "Luck or talent? Who cares if the end result is me taking all your money?"

"Look at them," one of the men says. "Bickering like an old married couple."

It could be my imagination but both Jan and Grandad look chagrined at this comment. Grandad clears his throat. "As soon as the boy gets here, we'll start."

The boy?

"Sorry I'm late!"

As if on cue, a voice sounds from around the corner and then a guy carrying a plastic container emerges. He is definitely not a boy. He's more like my age, but he's cuter than any of the guys who go to my school. He's tall, with dark hair that looks recently cut. Like all the beach locals, he's got an amazing tan. He's wearing black board shorts and a light blue T-shirt that hugs his chest in all the right ways. He sets the plastic food container on the table. "But I brought cookies."

One of the old guys pops the lid off and they all reach in and take a cookie. Jan takes two and hands one to me.

Grandad looks at me and I can't quite make out what he's thinking. Then again, I never can. "Jeremy, this is my granddaughter."

The guy turns toward me, and I see a long, jagged scar that cuts across his cheek. Luckily, I don't flinch or grimace or do anything stupid to express my shock at seeing that awful scar.

"Hi, there." Jeremy smiles and takes a seat across the table from me. He reaches for the deck of cards and begins shuffling it, and I notice another scar trailing down his forearm. It ends at the base of a beautiful tattoo of a dog paw that looks like a watercolor painting. I suddenly understand that old cliché about guys with scars being sexy. This guy is totally hot. Of course, he'd be hot without the scars too.

He looks at me and a shiver runs down my spine. "Are you the sweet granddaughter or the know-it-all stuck up one?"

I glance over at Grandad and find him smirking while eating his cookie. My dad is an only child, so the only two granddaughters are me and Kyndall. I can't believe this quiet, intimidating old man has talked about me to his friends.

"Er... the sweet one?"

"Cool." Jeremy expertly shuffles the deck of cards, and they make a satisfying *whoosh* sound. "Nice to meet you."

I glance over at Grandad again and he winks at me. I'm not sure what's crazier—that my broken heart is suddenly swooning over a guy I just met, or that my Grandad is smirking like he planned for this to happen.

FOUR

The passing of another week solidifies my new routine. I work on summer school and come out for meals and that's it. The only slight difference is that sometimes I'll gaze out of the French doors in my room and think about Jeremy. Not that it matters because he's just some guy I won't see again after the summer, but it's nice to have something else to think about besides my heartbreak.

One morning, Grandad suggests that I spend some time enjoying the beach, but I politely decline. The boredom of the last few days made me break down and check my cell phone more often and that's just brought me down lower than before. I am the laughing stock of my high school.

Destiny texts me occasionally and tells me not to worry. She says some other video will go viral soon and no one will care about me anymore. It's hard to believe her though because Lane's breakup video has over half a million views and it's only been two weeks. Plus, it's much easier to tell someone not to stress out when you're not the person on the video.

I ignore everyone but Destiny, and my dad, who calls once a day to check up on me, and I throw myself into my summer school work. Even with all the reading and videos and worksheets, I'm still not any better at Chemistry than I was before. This is a hard subject and my brain just doesn't get it. I'm not like Kyndall, Miss Straight A's her whole life. I'm not really good at anything, now that I think about it, and that just makes me more depressed.

In the morning, I wake up to the sound of metal scraping on metal, instead of the smell of bacon. I get dressed and venture into the small kitchen, finding Grandad bent inside the oven, a toolbox open on the floor.

"What's going on?" I ask.

He sits up and wipes his brow with the back of his hand. "Stove is broken. I've had it almost twenty years and it doesn't look like I can fix it. I guess it's about time for a new one."

"I'm sorry," I say as my stomach grumbles.

Grandad stands up and drops a wrench back in the toolbox. "Get some shoes on. Let's go out for breakfast."

I want to tell him that it's fine, I'll just eat cereal or toast or something, but Grandad isn't the kind of guy you want to disagree with. We head outside and get in his truck. This is the first time I've ever been in a car with my grandfather. Even after two weeks, it's still totally awkward because I've spent so much time alone in my room.

Luckily, the drive is a short one, and soon we're walking up to the Star diner, a retro-looking place that has a neon light in the window advertising that they're open twenty-four hours a day. The smell of breakfast and coffee makes my stomach rumble and I can't wait to eat something. We sit at the bar, on shiny red barstools, and order our food from a waitress that looks like she's trying really hard to fit the stereotype of "retro diner waitress." I dig it, though. Sterling Beach has this whole tourist town vibe and I kind of love it.

I also love that Grandad is a quiet person just like me. He sits next to me, sipping his coffee and he doesn't feel the need to chat incessantly or bother me with awkward small talk. This goes on peacefully for about three minutes, and then the smell of perfume washes over us.

"Look who it is!" Jan exclaims as she takes the barstool next to Grandad. "The world's worst poker player and his lovely granddaughter."

I laugh and Grandad just huffs. She had beaten him again last week, taking five dollars from him this time. They play with money, but only in quarters and dollar bills so the wagers are never too high.

"Well that's a little unfair," a voice says from beside

me. Jeremy slides onto the barstool next to me, bringing the scent of his earthy, citrusy body wash with him. "We don't know if he's the worst poker player in the *world*, but we do know he's the worst one in Sterling Beach."

He smiles at me and my heart jumps. I think I smile back.

The waitress brings our food and gives both Jan and Jeremy a look. "You two are so mean when you get together!"

Grandad chuckles. "It's all in good fun. For all they know, I lose on purpose to make them feel better."

Jeremy orders the French toast and asks our waitress to make sure that Hayes cooks it for him because apparently, he's the best cook on staff. After she brings his order to the back, a tall guy with a shaggy mop of curly hair pokes his head out from the kitchen and waves at Jeremy. They look about the same age, and since this is a small town, they've probably known each other forever. Something tells me the French toast thing is a frequent occurrence between them.

Beside me, Grandad is talking about his broken stove. Jan mentions that she can get him the family discount at an appliance store in town.

"But I'm not family," Grandad says.

"But I am," Jan says with a grin. "Come on, let's go now and they can have it installed for you by tomorrow. We can walk there."

He's finished with his breakfast, but I'm not, so I

don't really want to leave just yet. But he doesn't ask me to leave. Instead, leans over me to talk to Jeremy. "You mind taking her home?"

"Not at all," he says, flashing me a smile that makes my heart jump.

Grandad nods. "I'm going to go appliance shopping. See you later, Hadley. Have fun with Jeremy."

And then they just leave. Just like that, Jan and my grandfather walk outside and head to the appliance store, leaving me sitting here next to Jeremy. For all I know, he doesn't want to hang out with me. I can't believe Grandad did that.

"You don't have to hang out with me," I tell him quickly. Might as well let the super hot guy off the hook early.

He shoves a bite of French toast in his mouth and lifts an eyebrow. "You don't want to hang out with me?"

"No, I said... *you* don't have to hang out with *me*." My nerves are on overdrive right now. I still have half a plate of food left but I'm suddenly no longer hungry. When I look into Jeremy's eyes, all I can see are Lane's eyes that day when he dumped me while filming the whole thing. Boys can't be trusted. Maybe I should run outside and try to catch Grandad before it's too late.

"Yeah but—" Jeremy points his fork at me. "You would only say that if you didn't want to hang out with me."

I'm silent for a moment, wondering what on earth

I'm supposed to say to that. But then he cracks a grin and takes another bite. "I'm just messing with you. For spending the summer at a laid-back beach town, you are totally on edge all the time."

"I'm not on edge," I mutter, while I stir the scrambled eggs around on my plate. Of course, he's only seen me twice at poker nights and I spent both of those nights sitting quietly at the poker table.

Jeremy looks like he might want to disagree with me, but then he shrugs and goes back to eating. I try not to stare at his scar. It's not horrible or anything, just prominent. A long jagged slash of scar tissue that runs from just under his eye to the bottom of his sharp jawline. I want to ask where he got it, but I also don't want to be a jerk. I know first-hand that it's not fun having people ask you about something that was a bad experience.

"So where are you from?" he asks.

"Texas."

"Ah, cowboy land."

I roll my eyes. "All Texans aren't cowboys, you know. I've never even been on a horse."

He grins, and it makes his scar wrinkle in a way that's not so scary. "How long are you staying here?"

Some of my appetite has come back, so I take a bite of bacon. "My dad said I'll be here the whole summer, but I have this plan to beg him once a week to let me come home early. Maybe one of these days it'll work."

Just like Lane, Jeremy is also a fast eater. His plate

is empty just a few minutes after he got it. I take a deep breath and force the thoughts away. I might be in a total boy-hating mood right now, but it's still wrong to compare Jeremy to Lane. I'd bet all the coins on Grandad's poker table that Jeremy has never recorded himself breaking up with a girl just for the internet fame.

A little wrinkle forms between his brows while he studies me. "You make it sound like being here is a bad thing."

I shrug one shoulder. "It kind of is a bad thing."

"But you're at the beach! How could you not love it here?"

He's bringing up a good point. Normally I love the beach. Normally I love summer. But I'm not about to admit that right now. I shrug instead. "The beach is dumb."

He balks, putting a hand to his chest like I've just royally offended him. "Are you allergic to sunshine, sand and fun?"

"Maybe."

He frowns, and it looks cute on him. Actually, I'm pretty sure everything looks cute on him. "Is something bothering you?" He nudges me with his elbow and a sparkle of electricity floods through my body at his touch. "You can tell me if you want. I'm a great listener."

I try to give him a side-eyed glare, but when his eyes meet mine, I end up smiling. "You're a stranger."

"That makes me an even better listener." He reaches into his wallet and leaves a ten dollar bill on the table to cover his food.

"I don't really see the logic in that," I say, nodding to the waitress when she asks if I'm done with my food. Then I swivel in my barstool stool until I'm facing him. "Most people live by the philosophy that strangers are untrustworthy."

Jeremy bites his bottom lip, then runs a hand through his hair, making it stick out in sharp brown points before it sags back down again. I notice his arm tattoo for the second time. It's beautiful, like a real-life watercolor painting. Blues and purples and greens splash across his skin in the shape of a big dog paw print.

"Well, sure," he says, turning to face me. Our knees touch. "If you're talking about your regular run of the mill stranger, they're untrustworthy. But I'm not one of those strangers."

I cross my arms over my chest and give him a look. "How so?"

"I'm a close personal friend of your grandfather." Jeremy wiggles his eyebrows, knowing he's totally won this round. "He trusts me, so by extension, you should trust me too."

I open my mouth to retort something sarcastic, but I've got nothing. When Jeremy grins at me, there's this tiny little dimple in his left cheek. This is not good. I have moved beyond just admiring him as attractive. I'm totally crushing on him now. And that can't happen.

I clear my throat. "I don't need a ride home. I was actually hoping to get some exercise in, so I'll walk back."

He frowns. "You sure?"

I nod and play with the sugar packets on the bar. "Thanks anyway."

"Okay." He drums his fingertips on the table and then stands up. "Have a good day, Hadley."

I'm startled by his sudden desire to leave. I mean, don't get me wrong, I didn't want to hang out with him but now I kind of don't want him to leave. "Yeah, sure," I say trying not to look like I care. "You too."

He holds out one hand in a wave as he walks away. "See you tonight."

Tonight. It's Friday.

I don't know why his words, the promise of seeing me later, sends a shiver of nervous excitement through me. But I need to squash those feelings immediately. I'm not some fun, flirty girl eager for a summer fling. I've had my share of guys for the year. Maybe even for the whole decade. I can admire Jeremy's good looks from afar, but that's ALL I plan on doing. This stupid little crush ends now.

FIVE

I STARE AT THE LAPTOP SCREEN, MY HEART jumping around nervously in my chest. The final exam had been a fifty-question multiple choice test with an hour time limit. I finished with just a few seconds to spare. I read every question carefully, took my time, and did my best. And now, all I have to do is click on the link that says GRADE to know if I passed the exam, and thus passed my summer school course. If I did, I'll officially be a senior. If not... well, I don't want to think about that.

My teeth wear into my bottom lip and I move the mouse pointer over the link. I close my eyes and click.

87.

I got a B! More than a B... B plus!

I get off my bed and dance around my room. That 87 is the highest grade I've ever had on a chemistry test, and I have definitely earned it. Three weeks of sitting in this bedroom on my computer, working my butt off has totally been worth it. But it was so very hard. Hopefully I can go the rest of my life without ever doing chemistry again.

I fling open the bedroom door. "Grandad!" I call out.

"Yes?" he calls back.

It sounds like he's out on the porch which is where he spends a lot of his time, sitting alone and watching the ocean, occasionally reading a book or the newspaper. I go outside and feel the mid-afternoon sunshine on my face, smell the clean, fresh ocean air. "I passed my Chemistry class," I tell him.

His stoic expression shifts into a slight smile. "Good for you. You worked hard on it."

With my quick burst of excitement over, I realize I've never talked to him about my summer school. I know he knows about it, because my dad told him, but this is suddenly very awkward.

"Okay well, I just wanted to tell someone." I smile at him and then slip back inside. My grandad isn't as scary as I used to think he was, but he's not exactly super friendly, either.

Back inside my room, I'm still bursting with joy over finally finishing all this stupid school work. I call my dad and tell him the great news.

"Good job, Hadley."

I stare out the windows in the French doors in my room, sad that I don't have a good view of the beach from here, just a great view of the house next door. "So, do you think I could come back home now?"

"Why would I think that?" Dad asks, the annoyance evident in his voice.

"I finished my summer school. I passed it. I've been punished enough, trust me."

"You seem to have forgotten that your failing grades weren't the only reason you were sent there for the summer. If you come home now, you'll be right back with the bad influences that made you go to your cousin's party."

My teeth clamp together. "Dad. I didn't party. I don't know how many times I have to say that. Why won't you believe me?"

"When you're a parent and you walk in on your teenage daughter passed out drunk, then you can tell me why I don't believe you."

I've never been drunk in my life. Not that it matters. I bet Grandad would believe me if the same thing happened here. I let out a frustrated groan.

"I'm not in the mood to listen to your backtalk," Dad says angrily. "Enjoy the rest of your summer and maybe you should think about what you did and how you can take steps to behave better when you get back home."

He hangs up and I toss my phone on the bed in frustration. I am not a bad person. I'm not a bad friend, and I wasn't a bad girlfriend. I might suck at chemistry but that's all. I don't drink or do drugs or party. I've never snuck out of my house or lied to my dad or anything and yet I'm being treated like one of those terrible kids who go on talk shows and scream at their parents.

I just want to be home in my own town, in my own house, in my own bed. Not this stupid room that has all of my dad's old stuff in it, including his uncomfortable super ancient twin bed.

I drop to the bed and reach out for my phone as the reality of my situation settles over me. Ever since I got here, I wanted to go home. But home isn't exactly great right now, either. Home is where my step sister is constantly better than I am. It's where all the people at my school are still laughing over my breakup. It's where my ex-boyfriend is, reveling in all his newfound internet fame. I had planned out a wonderful summer with him before he broke up with me. We were going to go on romantic dates and watch the stars at night and go swimming in his backyard pool. I was so excited for summer to get here so that we could hang out more.

And all he was excited about was dumping me on live video.

"Hadley," Grandad calls out. "You have a visitor."

A *what?*

For the briefest second, I imagine that Lane is here, with a camera crew and they tell me I was the star on a TV show about pranking girlfriends into thinking they were dumped on TV. But of course, that's not going to happen. Even if it did, I don't think any amount of apology would make me forgive Lane for what he did.

I venture out into the living room to see what Grandad is talking about. I shouldn't be surprised when I see the tanned, gorgeous guy with mysterious scars standing there. He's got that beachy surfer look going on, like always. This time he's wearing red board shorts and a white T-shirt that has the sleeves cut off, revealing sculpted muscles and another scar at the top of his shoulder.

"Hey," he says, flashing me a quick smile. "I have a slight emergency and I really need your help."

I lift an eyebrow. "What kind of help can I give?"

"Don't be rude," Grandad says. "Go help the boy."

Not wanting to get on his bad side, I slip on the sandals I keep by the front door and follow Jeremy outside. He doesn't say anything as he jogs down the stairs.

"Is everything okay?" I ask, following him down to the driveway.

"Hopefully," he says. "I just really need your help."

There's a teal scooter motorcycle thing parked next to Grandad's truck. It looks like it's seen better days. The paint is worn and chipped, and the leather seat is cracked. Its only redeeming quality is that the wheels look brand new. Jeremy hands me the helmet that's hanging from the handlebars.

I take a step back. "I am not riding that thing."

He holds the helmet closer to me. "It only goes 40 miles an hour."

"You can die at much slower speeds," I say.

When he smirks he's so cute you barely even notice the scar on his cheek. "I'm a good driver. I promise."

"I guess if it's an emergency..." I say as I take the helmet and lower it over my head.

He nods. "It's an emergency."

I reach for the little straps that hang down by my chin, but I can't get them to click together at the buckle. Jeremy steps forward, a cute smile playing on his lips. "Is this your first time wearing a helmet?"

I consider it for a moment. "I think so."

He grins. "May I?"

I nod. He steps closer, bringing the amazing scent of his cologne with him. He smells like summertime. I watch him while he tilts the angle of the helmet, adjusting it to fit properly on my head. Then he takes the straps and moves them together, his fingers leaving a trail of goosebumps as they graze my skin. The buckle clicks together, and he takes a step back, his hands falling away from my face. "There we go."

I swallow. I don't know why the close contact felt so powerful just now. Maybe because I've been almost completely alone for the last three weeks.

He climbs on the scooter and starts it up. The motor is quiet and wimpy-sounding and it relaxes some of my fears. It's not like this thing is a race-worthy street bike. He looks back at me. "Ready?"

"Where's your helmet?" I ask.

"I only have the one."

I frown. "That's not safe."

"As long as my passenger is safe, we're all good."

Something in the way he says it makes my heart flutter. This random guy cares about my well-being more than my own boyfriend did. I bite back my anxiety of riding on a motorcycle and I climb onto the back. I've seen enough movies and motorcycles in real life to know that the person on the back has to hold onto the driver so they don't fall off. But the idea of wrapping my arms around Jeremy makes me more nervous than the idea of riding a motorcycle. But I don't want to fly off the back of this thing, so I grab onto his sides.

A few minutes later, I don't know what I was worried about. The scooter is not fast at all. I feel like I could be pedaling a bicycle and still keep up with him. I relax as we turn out of the neighborhood and onto the main road. The beautiful beach is on our right, and to our left are tons of beach houses and the occasional gas station or surf shop. The south side of Sterling Beach is more residential, and I remember from my trips here as a kid that the north end of the beach is the tourist area with a boardwalk and lots of souvenir shops.

As we ride along, we pass some beautiful houses that could probably be called beach mansions. I take in their beauty as much as the beauty of the beach on the other side of the road. Since it's summer, the beach is filled with families, surfers, and even some dogs on long leashes.

I close my eyes, my arms around Jeremy's waist to keep me steady, and I take in the smell of the ocean, the feeling of the warm summer sun on my skin. Maybe being here isn't so bad at after all.

We ride all the way to the touristic boardwalk and come to a stop at a bright blue building with crisp white trim. Murdoch's Gift Shop is engraved on the wooden sign above the door. Jeremy parks the bike and I climb off. Even in the warm summer sun, my body feels cold with all the space between us now.

I'm able to take off the helmet on my own, but a silly part inside of me kind of wants to ask for his help. I take a deep breath and try to stop thinking of his fingers on my cheek.

"So what's the emergency?" I say, looking around. The gift shop isn't on fire or anything. There are no screaming people fleeing from a shark in the waters. Everything is calm and normal.

Jeremy smooths down his windswept hair. "We need to get a souvenir for my little nephew. He's seven and he already has a bunch of Sterling Beach T-shirts, so maybe something else, but it needs to have the Sterling Beach logo on it."

I put my hands on my hips. "You need help picking out a gift for a little kid?"

"Yep," he says, all matter-of-factly. "My sister and brother-in-law come down here every summer but this year they got stuck working and can't visit, and my nephew is devastated about it. I want to get him a gift to cheer him up."

"That's not an emergency."

He smirks. "I never said the emergency was mine."

I throw my hands up in the air. "So who's emergency is it?"

"Yours." He starts walking toward the gift shop and I run to catch up with him.

"How exactly am I having an emergency right now?"

He holds open the door for me, but I stop short, staring at him for an answer.

"You've been cooped up in that house for weeks now. I haven't seen you on the beach at all, and that's just not right. Mr. Clint says you refuse to come out of your room, and well, that's an emergency. I thought I would try to cheer you up."

I can think of about one million ways to argue with him right now, but the softness in his eyes tells me he didn't lie to me to be mean. He just genuinely wants to make my summer a little brighter.

"You could have just asked me," I say as I walk into the gift shop. "I would have come with you."

He falls in step with me. "Good to know."

SIX

THE RIDE BACK HOME FEELS TOO SHORT. As soon as I see Grandad's house in the distance, I'm suddenly not ready to get off the scooter again. I certainly don't want to go back up to my room. I might not admit this to Jeremy but getting out of the house today had been a great idea. We walked all around the gift shop, played with the hermit crabs, and picked out matching neon green sunglasses. I put them on just for fun but Jeremy had insisted on buying us both a pair.

I'm wearing them now as we ride back home, the shopping bag filled with Jeremy's nephew's gift tucked in the crook of my arm. My other arm is wrapped around his side. I try to keep my grip as loose as possible but occasionally we hit a bump in the road and I can feel the ripples of his abs. Lane did *not* have abs like this.

Not that it matters, I tell myself. Lane is no longer my boyfriend and Jeremy never will be.

My grandad stands at the top of the stairs when we arrive. I wonder how long he's been there, if he's keeping tabs on me. Or maybe it was just a coincidence.

Jeremy stops, but keeps the motor running. I want to ask him to stay a while but I can't find the words to say it, so I just climb off the scooter. "Thanks for the emergency fix," I say, smiling at him. Our sunglasses have an orange-blue mirror tint to the lenses and I can see myself in the reflection while I look at him.

"Anytime."

He looks like he might want to say more, but then he looks up instead, and waves at Grandad. "Thanks for letting me borrow your granddaughter."

"You hungry?" he calls out.

"Always," Jeremy says.

Grandad nods. "You can stay for dinner. I'm grilling ribs. They'll be ready in about an hour."

"Sounds good, sir."

Grandad nods once and then walks off, presumably back to the grill at the other end of the porch. Jeremy turns off the scooter. "You know... I don't think we've fully fixed your emergency," he says.

"Oh yeah?" My heart jumps for joy. Maybe our little hang out session doesn't have to end so soon. "What else do we need to do?"

His hand reaches behind his head and he stares up

at me. I'm the taller one now that he's sitting on the scooter and I'm standing. He gives me an unsure grin. "Walk on the beach?"

I grin right back at him. "Sounds fun."

We walk to the edge of Grandad's property, where the grass thins and then becomes sand. My dad always talks about how he could sell this place and make a lot of money because it's right on the ocean and ocean properties are highly coveted. My grandad always says that my dad can do whatever he wants with the place after he's dead. I know Dad will probably want to sell it right away when that fateful day comes, but right now as I'm standing here, gazing out at the beautiful Atlantic Ocean, a super cute guy standing next to me, I wonder if I could convince my dad to keep it. Maybe even let me live here one day.

I take a step forward and Jeremy grabs my hand. "Wait!"

I look at him, unable to speak because he's *holding my hand*, and it's making my whole body feel fuzzy and warm.

He releases my hand and kicks off his shoes. "You can't wear sandals on the beach."

"You can't?" My voice is back, now that we're not touching. Funny how this boy can render me mute just like that. I follow his lead and kick off my sandals.

He shakes his head. "No way. You don't get the full beach walk experience if you're wearing shoes."

"Good point."

Jeremy chuckles. "This might be a bigger emergency than I originally thought. Hadley, have you ever been to the beach?"

I give him a playful punch in the arm. "Yes," I say sarcastically. "We have a beach at home. It's about an hour drive from my house and we go in the summer sometimes."

The sand squishes under my feet as we walk out toward the water. Unlike in the northern part of the city where all the tourists and hotels are, this beach is more secluded. The property owners don't actually own the beach—the property line stops right where the sand starts—but I've noticed that people don't really hang out here unless they live nearby.

He shoves his hands in his pockets as walk. "How do Texas beaches compare with Virginia?"

"You guys have way prettier beaches," I admit. "We have the Gulf of Mexico and the sand is all muddy brown and covered in dead seaweed. The water is the same color."

"Bummer." He walks close to the water's edge, letting his feet get wet every time the water rolls to the shore. "At least you have this beach. Are you still stuck here for the whole summer?"

I shrug and kick at a seashell. "I think so. I haven't had any luck in begging my dad to let me go home."

"Why do you want to go home so badly?" There's a gentle hesitation in his question, something that hangs in the air and makes me feel like he's looking for a very specific answer. Like I'm trying to get home to something. Or someone.

I shrug. "Honestly? I don't even know. My dad is mad at me. My friends are stupid. My cousin let me take the fall for something I didn't even do." I kick at the sand again, but an incoming wave washes away my anger, leaving smooth sand in its wake. "Don't even get me started on my stepsister."

"Go ahead and talk about her," he says. "I'm a good listener."

I shake my head. That's the second time he's told me that, but I still don't feel comfortable talking too much about too many personal things. "No. I can't let her ruin my summer. She's not worth it."

"Agreed," he says with a nod. "Life is too short to let anything stress you out."

I laugh so suddenly I snort. "Please. You sound like a greeting card."

"It's true."

I roll my eyes. "I hate to break it to you, Jeremy, but there are tons of things worth stressing out about."

Jeremy's tongue slides over his bottom lip. "Name three."

My cheeks redden. The first thing that comes to mind is getting dumped on YouTube. But I can't say that out loud. "Just... trust me," I say, letting out a deep breath. "Life is stressful."

"It doesn't have to be. Every day is a gift, Hadley. You just have to see it like that, realize the precious value of what you've been given every day, and then little things that used to stress you out will feel like nothing."

"Okay… you should definitely get a job writing greeting cards. I bet Hallmark would hire you in a heartbeat."

His lips turn up in one corner. "You think I'm being cheesy."

I shrug. "Maybe a little bit."

He accepts my words and doesn't act like they bother him. We walk in silence for a few steps and then I start feeling angsty. "Surely something stresses you out," I say softly, looking over at him.

He draws in a deep breath, his shoulders straightening. Then he lets it out slowly and shakes his head. "Nope."

"Oh, please," I say, bumping into him with my elbow. "Everyone is stressed about something."

Those dark blue eyes flit over, his contemplative gaze penetrating me. I've only been around Jeremy a few times, but every single time, it feels like there are things he's not saying. Things he wants to say, things that might even be on the tip of his tongue, but I never get to hear them. Is he holding back for his sake, or mine?

"What is it?" I say, my voice barely a breath. "I can tell you're thinking something."

His lips quirk up just a little bit. He's walking on my right side, so I can't see the scar that mars his otherwise beautiful face. "I'm thinking a lot of things," he says.

I swallow. Again, there's something he's not saying. "I'm a good listener."

"It's interesting," he says, taking a hand out of his pocket to run it through his hair. "Talking to someone my age who doesn't know me... that hasn't happened since the accident."

Okay. I can feel it. The weight of whatever is on his shoulders has been revealed.

"Accident?" I say so softly the ocean waves carry it away and I don't know if he heard me. I know without a doubt he's talking about whatever gave him those scars.

He looks down at his feet while we walk, his toes curling into the wet sand with every step. "It was last year. Valentine's Day, actually."

My stomach clenches. I might have promised to be a good listener but talking about an old girlfriend isn't high on my list of conversation topics.

"I only remember that because the hospital was full of pink and red decorations."

The knots in my stomach loosen. Okay, so no girlfriend story. "What happened?"

"It was late, around nine o'clock. I was walking my dog like I always did, but we couldn't walk on the beach like normal."

He looks over at me and curls his lip. "Valentine's

Day makes couple do some gross things on the sand when they think it's too dark for anyone to notice."

"Ew," I say.

He nods. "So, I took Buddy on the road for his walk. And... well... I had my earbuds in listening to music and I didn't hear the car coming. It was a drunk driver, and he veered off the road and took us out." He swallows hard, looking down at his right arm. Not at the scar, I realize, but at the tattoo.

"Buddy died on impact. I, uh...I survived, but there was a long time where I wished I hadn't."

"Oh my God," I breathe. Tears flood my eyes as images of a poor dog lying dead on the road, Jeremy next to it clinging to life.

"I'll spare you the gory details, but now I have sixteen pins and screws in my arm and shoulder. I had to have three surgeries on my face to fix my eye socket." He turns to face me, and my eyes are drawn immediately to his scarred cheek. "Believe it or not, this thing looks really good for what happened to me."

"It doesn't look bad at all," I say, and I realize I mean it. It was a little jarring at first, but now that I know him, I barely notice it.

"I didn't know pain like that was possible," he says. "I wanted to die. I prayed to die. I was stuck lying on the road holding my dead dog for two hours before someone drove by and saw me. The deadbeat degenerate who hit me was found miles away after he ran into a telephone pole and totaled his car." He snorts sarcastically. "He had no injuries."

I put a hand on his arm. "Jeremy, I'm so sorry."

"Don't be," he says, offering me a small smile. "It made me the person I am. For as much as I wanted to die, I didn't. I survived. And now..." he shrugs his shoulders and reaches for my hand, giving it a squeeze. "Now I don't see things the way I used to. A stubbed toe, a traffic jam—nothing really bothers me anymore. Because I'm alive and that means I have the privilege to experience all of life. The good and the bad."

"You are such a better person than I am," I say.

He chuckles. "You seem like a great person to me."

His eyes meet mine and I'm overcome with emotions. Grief for what he's been through, inspiration for what he's learned about life. He's suffered through something unimaginable. All I did was get dumped and fail a class.

At some point in this conversation we stopped walking. Now we're facing the water, and I notice the cool rush of it flooding over the tops of my feet. I wrap my hand around his arm and lower my head to his shoulder. "I'm sorry about your dog."

"Thanks," he says, letting his head lower on top of mine. "Buddy would have loved you."

I don't know what comes over me, but it's a heavy feeling. Warm and comfortable and strong, like a blanket that settles over my shoulders and makes everything feel different somehow. We stand like this for a long while, watching the ocean dance under the beautiful blue sky.

"Hadley?" Jeremy says softly.

I look up at him. "Yes?"

He grins. The fading afternoon sunlight sparkles in his eyes, bathing him in a golden glow that makes him look even cuter than usual.

"Can I kiss you?"

My eyes widen. This is the last thing I expected him to say, but as soon as he says it, I realize it's exactly what I want. My teeth press down on my bottom lip. I nod slowly.

His hand reaches up, his fingertips touching my cheek so lightly that I want to tilt my head and press into him. But I hold absolutely still as he takes a step closer to me. The ocean ripples water onto our feet. I am aware of the cool rush of water, the warm blazing feeling of his fingertips on my cheek, the intoxicating smell of his cologne. The blue of his eyes, so impossibly deep and filled with sincerity.

And then they close, and mine close too, and Jeremy places the softest kiss on my lips. My breath catches in my throat. I hold onto this perfect, sweet moment for as long as I can. When his lips break away, he tilts his forehead to mine.

It wasn't a passionate, or wild kiss. It was sweet, gentle. Perfect.

Maybe it's what we both needed.

Everything seems to have changed overnight. I went from hating Sterling Beach to loving it. After my long walk on the beach with Jeremy, he'd started to feel like someone I can trust. And yeah, I can't lie and say I'm not totally crushing on him, but that part doesn't matter. He can be extremely cute and adorable but still be just a friend. I know better than to try to get in a relationship right now, even if it's just a summer fling. All guys do is hurt you. I'm not going to get hurt again. Nope. Not me.

Maybe I just needed a friend. Maybe that's all it took to make me wake up this morning feeling like everything might possibly be okay. I still have to go back home at the end of summer and face everyone at school next year and be constantly compared to my stepsister Kyndall around my family, but maybe it'll all be okay. I can get through this because I know something I didn't know before—the world is huge. There is more to life than small town Texas high school drama. I can move away; I can make new friends.

I've only had the idea for a few hours, so I haven't said anything to Grandad yet. For all I know, he might be completely against the idea but something tells me he might be receptive to it. We may not talk much, but we get along well. Over the last few days I've started to help him cook dinner and clean up around the house. We each keep to ourselves, except for poker nights, where we hang out with his friends. Maybe this could become a long-time thing. Maybe I could move out here after graduation, go to college in Virginia, and make all new friends, starting with Jeremy.

I can hear Grandad moving around in the kitchen, the sound of him setting the frying pan on the stove, and the *click, click, click* of the gas stove heating up. He loves his new appliance even though it's sleek and modern and doesn't fit in with the rest of the kitchen at all.

I join him in the kitchen and start making a pot of coffee.

"You're going to need more scoops than that," he says, nodding toward the coffee filter.

"It's four cups," I say, furrowing my brows. "I always make four cups."

"That's when we don't have company coming over."

"Who's coming over?" I ask, unable to hide my smile. "Is it Jan?"

Last night when Jeremy and I had returned from our walk, we found Jan and Grandad sitting on the porch together, eating cookies she had brought, even though he hadn't had dinner yet. I think it's pretty obvious that Jan has a thing for my Grandad.

"No." He rips open a package of bacon and gives me a look. "Your family is almost here. Didn't they tell you?"

My family?

Right then, there's a loud knock on the door. I walk over an answer it, surprised to see Dad, Lucy, and Kyndall all standing there with suitcases.

"What are you doing here?" I ask, stunned to see them after so long. A week ago, I might have hoped Dad was here to take me back home. But now I kind of wish they'd all stay back in Texas and let me enjoy my newfound life.

"Well that's a rude hello," Dad says, brushing past me. "I told you we were coming up for a weekend visit."

"No, you didn't."

Lucy's lips flatten into a disapproving line as she walks inside, her teenage look-alike right behind her. Kyndall doesn't even acknowledge me. I guess now that she's going to Harvard, she's too good to talk to pathetic losers like me.

"I called you and left a voicemail," Dad says. "I also texted you."

"Oops." I don't even remember the last time I looked at my phone. With all the constant reminders of Lane and the breakup, my once beloved phone has become completely worthless to me.

I hadn't realized how much my grandad had warmed up to me until my family sits at the kitchen table and he goes all cold and intimidating again. It occurs to me now that maybe the tough old veteran isn't just a mean guy... maybe he just doesn't like my dad and stepmom. After all, Dad hasn't been here three minutes before he starts talking about how he could help find a real estate agent to sell the place.

Somehow, we make it through breakfast. I take a lesson from my grandad and just keep my mouth shut as much as I can. Kyndall and Lucy fill the conversation with talks of themselves, mostly about Harvard. After breakfast, everyone goes to sit on the porch and soak up the morning sun, and I slip off to my bedroom to check my phone. The battery is dead so after a few minutes of charging it, it finally turns on.

Messages and notifications flood onto my screen. Sure enough, there's a text from Dad, sent three days ago. *We decided to come visit for the weekend. Don't get any ideas, you're not coming home early.*

I roll my eyes and then skim through the other messages. Most of my missed calls and texts are from my cousin Destiny. All I see at first are tons of exclamation marks because she's clearly freaking out about something and she wants me to call her immediately.

I still haven't totally forgiven her for having that stupid house party that got me in trouble, but she is my cousin and also my best friend, so I give her a call.

"Oh my God, you're alive!"

"Hello to you too," I say with a snort as I sit on my bed. "What's going on?"

"Hadley, what the crap?" she says, sounding all in a panic. "Have you gotten any of my messages? Do you know? Are you pissed? Are you okay?"

"Whoa… take a deep breath," I say. "I've been busy here and I haven't been on my phone. I don't know anything about back home but if it's about that stupid video, I don't care."

"It's not totally about the video," she says. I hear her sigh deeply into the phone. "But it is about Lane."

My chest constricts. "I don't care about Lane," I say, and I really do mean it. He dumped me in a cruel way and my feelings for him are totally gone.

"I know but, it's also about Kyndall."

My blood runs cold. "What about her?"

"Well…" My cousin is suddenly at a loss for words, and that's pretty much impossible. I should check outside and make sure pigs aren't flying. She takes a deep breath. "Lane's newest video has Kyndall in it… and… well… it's pretty obvious that they're dating."

All the air whooshes out of my lungs. My face actually feels numb for a second, and then I take a deep breath. "Are you kidding me?"

"I wish I was," she says. "I'm so sorry. I wanted you to hear it from me and not see it on some stupid social media post... Hadley, I'm so sorry."

"It's fine," I say, but it's definitely not fine. I hang up the phone and stand, my legs feeling both wobbly and angry at the same time. Maybe it's from all the anger that's coursing through my body. Kyndall and I aren't exactly best friends but I can't fathom how she could do something like this to me.

Anger and humiliation take over and before I realize what I'm doing, I've marched through the house and to the porch. My family sits on the wicker furniture, and they all look over at me.

"Are you dating Lane?"

My voice is sharp and unwavering, cutting through the stunned silence like a knife. "Answer me," I say, stopping right in front of my stepsister. "Because the whole internet seems to think that you are."

Her jaw stiffens. My stepsister, who I've known almost all of my life, looks me right in the eye and says, "You clearly already know the answer."

I am so, so glad that I don't burst into tears. Instead, I let all of the betrayal and anger boil up inside of me and I focus on those feelings instead. They make me strong, not weak.

"You're a terrible person," I say, my voice ice cold.

"Hadley," my dad says sternly, but I ignore him.

"It's just a boy," Lucy says with that stupid laugh of hers that always makes me feel less than. She clucks her tongue. "I can't believe you're this upset over a boy. You're not even dating him anymore."

"It's not my fault," Kyndall says with a shrug. "I told him the breakup video would be kind of mean but he didn't listen."

"You *knew*?" She flinches at how loud I'm yelling. "You knew he was going to do that and you didn't warn me? It's bad enough that you stole my boyfriend but this breaks every single girl code. You're a terrible person!"

"Hadley!" my dad says again, this time with a sharpness in his voice that makes me flinch.

Lucy puts a hand on his arm. "Honey you know this is how she is. Totally immature and irrational. Don't let it stress you out."

My nostrils flare. If I wouldn't get grounded for all of eternity, I would totally slap my stepmother right about now. Instead, I look at Kyndall, who is sitting there in Grandad's favorite patio chair, looking down her nose at me.

"I wonder what Harvard would say if they knew how terrible you are."

Lucy mutters something sarcastic, but I don't bother paying attention. I turn and head straight for the stairs, and then I jog down them, two at a time, as fast as humanly possible. Dad calls my name again but I ignore it. When I get to the road, I run. And run. I run until my bare feet feel blistered and sore, and my lungs are about to explode from breathing so heavily. I run until it's safe enough to cry.

EIGHT

I don't know how much time passes, but it's probably hours. I have no phone or watch to tell the time, but I can tell when the sun is no longer directly overhead, so I know it's probably past noon. I've already cried myself out, and now I just feel tired. Overwhelmed. And mad at myself. I'm so mad at how I cried like that. I don't like Lane anymore. I never even loved him. We hadn't dated long enough for that, but it still hurts. It hurts that he humiliated me, it hurts that my stepsister is an evil witch, and it hurts that my dad looks at me like I'm some delinquent terrible person that he regrets being related to.

Everything just hurts. For a very short while, being with Jeremy made it all better, but now as I sit here on the sand, my back leaning against a large rock, I realize that kissing Jeremy was the biggest mistake I've made all summer. I let myself forget about reality. I wanted to escape into him, wrap myself up in his arms, and pretend like everything is fine. But it's not fine.

Jeremy is sweet and kind and crazy hot. But he lives a thousand miles away. He might be a fun distraction, but after the summer is over, he'll be here and I'll be back in Texas. Kissing him was so stupid.

I lean my head back against the large rock and close my eyes. It's not comfortable but it's big enough to provide some shade from the sun and privacy from all the happy people on the beach. When I left Grandad's house I ran south, away from the tourist part of town but I didn't realize just how far down the beach houses go. There are miles and miles of beach houses dotted along the shore, and all of them are filled with people who are outside enjoying the summer. Good. At least some people can have fun right now.

"Mind if I join you?"

My eyes fly open at the sound of his familiar voice. Jeremy stands here, his lean body casting a shadow over my face. He's barefoot, like always, and wearing tan shorts with a green T-shirt. I recognize the logo on his shirt from one of the surf shops on Main Street.

"Go for it," I say.

He sinks into the sand next to me. "So... I take it family time isn't going so well?"

"How did you know?"

"I live next door," he says as if that part was obvious. "I heard some of it from my porch."

I sink my head into my hands. "Oh, God."

"Your sister is kind of a brat."

"*Step*-sister." I look over at him. "And whatever makes you think that?" I say sarcastically.

He chuckles. "I heard her complaining from the second they parked. She doesn't want to be there, but now I guess it's because she's stole your boyfriend or something?"

Heat flushes through my whole body. "She didn't steal him," I say, and I realize I don't exactly know if that's true. Maybe she did. "We were already broken up but she knew he was going to break up with me and she didn't tell me. And now..." I wave my hand through the air. "I guess they're dating. Whatever. I don't care."

"I'm sorry."

"It's nothing," I say as I stare out at the ocean.

"Did you love him?"

His question is jarring, and when I look over at him, I see concern in his eyes. Maybe even worry. I smile. "No. Not even a little bit."

"Cool," he says, returning my grin. "I mean I'm not jealous or anything but..."

I laugh. "Are you saying you like me?"

"Oh, I'm *way* past liking you."

I really hope all this time outside has made me sunburned because all the blood in my body just rushed to my cheeks.

"You're really cute when you're embarrassed," Jeremy says.

"Shut up." I smack his arm. "I'm not embarrassed.

What are you even doing way out here?"

"Looking for you."

I let my fingers sink into the sand. "Why were you looking for me?"

"I could tell you were hurt and I didn't want you to be hurt. I saw the direction you ran but I had to get clothes on and by the time I was downstairs, I couldn't find you."

"You were sitting on your porch naked?" I ask, desperate to change the subject away from my personal problems.

Now it's his turn to blush. "No... I was wearing pajama pants."

"You didn't have to spend all this time looking for me," I say, running my hands over the soft white sand. "I'm fine."

"No, you're not, Hadley. You're hurting."

"Jeremy..." I heave a sigh. "I'm fine."

His hand grabs mine, stopping it from sliding around in the sand. He turns it over and links his fingers through mine, then meets my gaze. "I promised that life is more fun than it seems, and I'm going to prove it to you."

A mischievous look dances in his gaze. "Let's go."

I'm weary from all the crying, and my hair and skin feel salty from sitting on the beach so long, but when Jeremy reaches out his hand to me, I want more than anything to grab it. So, I do.

We walk hand in hand along the beach, passing all

the beach-goers, surfers, sunbathing beauties, and children making sand castles. Jeremy doesn't say anything, and I'm grateful for the silence. All I need is to be around him and I feel better.

After a while, I notice Grandad's house in the distance. I can't see anyone on the porch, but I'm sure my family is still there, maybe sitting inside and sharing stories about what a horrible person I am for running out on them. The house before Grandad's is white with blue trim, and the house on the other side is a soft pastel yellow.

"Which house is yours?" I ask.

"The yellow one," Jeremy says. "I've lived there my whole life."

"Do you like it here?"

He nods. "It's a nice, quiet town."

"How's your school?"

"SBH is all right. I mean, I don't have anything else to compare it to, I suppose."

"Are you popular?" I say, giving him a teasing grin. "A super-hot guy like you is probably at the top of the high school popularity ladder."

"Nah," he says, shaking his head. "I mean, maybe more than I used to be. The accident kind of brought the whole community together. Suddenly everyone knew my name and they had fundraising events in the newspaper and stuff. But after I finished physical therapy, all that fame kind of wore off."

"At least you're not famous in a bad way," I say,

suddenly feeling nauseous. Before he can ask what I mean about that, I change the subject. "So where are we going? Please tell me we aren't going home."

"Nope. Somewhere better. Somewhere delicious."

We walk a little further, up to where the south beach officially becomes the fancy private beach. There is a wooden fence that separates the beach, going all the way out into the water. You could hop over it if you wanted, but the imposing mansions that face the water are intimidating enough for me to stay away from their part of the beach.

At the fence, Jeremy turns left and walks up to the land. "We're almost there," he says, squeezing my hand.

We get to the main road, where shops and tourists abound. There are people everywhere, enjoying the quaint town with all of the activities it has to offer. I feel self-conscious, the loser girl from Texas, while I'm holding Jeremy's hand. I expect him to let me go once we're around people, but he doesn't. Isn't he afraid of his friends seeing me? I'm not cute right now. My eyes are swollen from crying, and I'm wearing an old pair of cut off shorts and a baggy T-shirt that I slept in last night. I am so far from cute it's a little ridiculous.

"Here we are," Jeremy says, stopping in front of one of the little shops. I can smell the pies before I see them, and I look up at the sign over the door. Aunt Mary's Pie Shop. "Hope you like pie."

"I love pie," I say with a grin. I haven't eaten

anything all day, so at this point I'd take any food offered, but pie seems amazing.

The mouth-watering smells of sugary goodness make my stomach rumble the moment we step inside. The place is small, with a few round tables that seat two people, and it's packed to the brim with customers.

"The apple pie is amazing. And the cherry pie is, too." Jeremy talks excitedly about all twelve flavors of pie that are offered by the slice. "And of course, you can't go wrong with chocolate."

"How am I supposed to choose?" I say. "You're making them all sound good."

"So, let's get all of them," he says, wiggling his eyebrows as we approach the counter.

"We can't get twelve pies," I say.

"Sure, we can." He winks at me and then looks at the woman behind the counter. "Can we get a sampler?"

"Sure thing, Jeremy." The older woman smiles warmly at us and then turns around and grabs a pie tin. It has one slice of each of the twelve pies the shop offers. That's actually genius. "You need two forks?" she asks, smiling at me.

"Yes ma'am." Jeremy takes his wallet out of his back pocket, but the woman slides the pie closer to him and shakes her head.

"No charge. We love seeing you here. And it's even better that you brought a beautiful young lady with you."

"Ignore her," Jeremy says. "She makes it her life goal to embarrass me."

"Oh, and I'm so good at it!" The woman says with a hearty chuckle. She hands two plastic forks to me and then leans forward, pretending to whisper even though she's not whispering at all. "He's a keeper, honey. I promise."

"Thanks," I say, glancing up at Jeremy. "I had a feeling he might be."

We find a small empty table tucked into the corner and make our way over to it just as a bunch of teenage guys walk in. "Jeremy!" one of them calls out while the other three guys walk up to the counter to order. "Nice to see you, man. Haven't seen you since school got out."

"What's up?" Jeremy fist-bumps his friend. "Good to see you, too. What's been going on?"

"Surfing, boarding, the usual deal. We've just been carving it up this morning and now it's time for some eats. You know how grumpy Hayes gets when he's hungry." Jace winks, hooking his thumb toward the tall guy with shaggy hair that's ordering pie. I recognize him as the cook who makes the best French toast.

"I'm going to go wash my hands," I say, slipping out of their conversation and to the bathroom. I'm starving and I'm so ready to dive into tasting twelve different types of pie. I wash my hands and try not to freak out at my reflection in the small framed mirror. My hair is a total mess, so I take it out of its ponytail and try to wrangle it into a cute messy bun. It's better, but not by much. My bare face would look a lot better with some mascara and lip gloss, but at least it's not sunburned. Oh well. I guess I can't do much about my appearance right now. And Jeremy has already seen me, and he still chose to hold my hand.

The woman behind the counter was right. He would be a total keeper if only I lived in Sterling Beach. With a sigh, I leave the bathroom and notice that the guys are all standing around the small table. They can't possibly want to sit with us because there's not enough chairs, so what are they doing?

One of the guys is holding out his cell phone, showing something to everyone else. Jeremy looks on right next to Hayes.

"Dude, he just breaks up with her," the guy with the phone says. "You can tell she totally wasn't expecting it. There's no way this is a skit. It has to be real."

My heart stops. My breath catches in my throat. And then, across the small restaurant, all other sounds fade away until the only thing I hear is Lane's voice talking as the video begins. We're a thousand miles away from home but the worst day of my life has made it here to Sterling Beach. And Jeremy is going to see it all.

I don't have any tears left to cry. But I do know one thing I'm still good at.

Running away.

NINE

My family doesn't stay long after the one-sided yelling match. They left the very next day, which is fine by me. I don't want to see anyone right now, especially not my stepsister.

Days later, I hear my granddad answer the door, then say the same thing he's said for the last four days. "Sorry son, she's not feeling well. I'll let her know you stopped by."

This must be what people did before cell phones existed. When they had to actually show up at someone's house, day after day, if they wanted to talk. The way it is now, people just call or text you a million times until you reply. But Jeremy doesn't have my phone number. In all the times we've hung out over the last few weeks, there was never a need to share phone numbers. He would just show up and I'd be here.

Ghosting someone on a cell phone is a lot easier

than in real life. I've had to keep to my room, telling Grandad I don't feel well, for four days now. I can't believe Jeremy is still coming by. Can't he take a hint? I am completely, horribly, irrevocably humiliated. I don't want to see him. I can't look into his eyes anymore now that he knows I'm a pathetic loser who got dumped on the internet. I wish he would just accept that and go away.

The great thing about Grandad is that he doesn't pry. I think he knows I'm not actually sick—like the stuffy nose, puking, fever type of sick—but he doesn't ask any questions. He brings me food and then carts away my empty dishes. He really is a great guy. Before I go home, I need to make sure I tell him that.

I spend another day in bed, watching the little TV in the corner, and avoiding the phone. My phone is connected to the internet and every time I look at it, I remember that stupid video. I want to live in a simpler time where the only technology is cable television and electricity and no one is humiliating other people for all the world to see.

As soon as my stomach starts to rumble for dinner, there's a light knock on my door. Grandad comes in, carrying a pizza box and two bottled sodas.

"You like pizza, right?"

I nod. "I love pizza."

"Good." He walks across my dad's old bedroom, to the glass doors that open out onto a balcony—only I've never been able to get them open. He reaches up and unhooks a lock at the top of the door. Weird. I've never even noticed that lock before. The doors swing open with ease.

"Let's eat out here," he says, setting the pizza box on the little end table that's between two patio chairs.

There are no plates or napkins. Grandad just opens the box and takes a slice of pizza with his hands. I do the same thing.

We eat in silence, staring out at the obscured view of the beach for two whole slices of pizza, and then he clears his throat and looks over at me. "What's going on, Hadley?"

"Um, nothing?" I say lightly, hoping he was asking in a lighthearted kind of way, not a we-need-to-talk kind of way.

"You've gone back to sulking in your room this week," he says, his expression stern but also kind. "I thought you were over this. What Kyndall did was stupid but you shouldn't let it bother you. You're such a better person than she is."

I guess he wasn't asking in a lighthearted way.

I shrug. "I don't care about her. I'm fine."

"You're not fine," he says. "Did Jeremy do something?"

I shake my head quickly. "No, he's great."

"Jeremy is a good kid. He's been through a lot. And he's clearly worried about you, so you staying in your room ignoring him is awfully rude if he didn't do anything to hurt you."

"I know…" I say, feeling guilt rise up in my throat. "I just… it's a long story."

Grandad reaches for another slice of pizza. "I have time. I'm retired. I have all the time in the world."

I swallow. Am I actually about to reveal my humiliating breakup to my grandfather who I barely know? My subconscious snorts sarcastically in my mind. *Who else are you going to tell? Your cousin screwed you over, your dad is mad at you, and all your friends at home are laughing at you.*

"Jeremy accidently saw a video on the internet. My boyfriend—well, ex-boyfriend, broke up with me and he filmed the whole thing and put it online."

Grandad's nostrils flare and he curses under his breath.

Now that I've started talking, I don't want to quit. Telling someone feels so much better than keeping it all to myself. "It was bad enough that my whole school saw it and is laughing at me, but the video got so popular that the guys in Sterling Beach saw it too, and they showed it to Jeremy when we were in town the other day. I got so embarrassed, I just came home and I haven't talked to him about it. I don't want to talk to him. I don't want to see him. It's too humiliating."

"Why do you think Jeremy should be punished for something another person did to you?" Grandad asks.

"I'm not punishing him," I say defensively.

Grandad's expression says otherwise. "You can say that all you want, but you haven't had to see the look on that poor kid's face every time I tell him you don't want to see him."

"But if I see him, he'll want to talk about it, and I don't want to talk about it."

"So tell him that," Grandad says. "He's a good kid. If you tell him you don't want to talk about it, he'll accept that."

"I guess you're right…" I say, feeling like total crap. "But I'm still horribly humiliated."

"So what?" Grandad snorts. "It happens to everyone. All you can do is overcome it and spend time with people who care about you. People who accept you for who you are."

"I like talking to you, Grandad." The words are out of my mouth before I realize it, and a blush comes to my cheeks. On the outside, he doesn't seem like someone who would be all friendly and happy to talk about problems. But once you get to know my grandad, that's exactly who he is. Hard and scary on the outside, but sweet and caring on the inside.

"I like talking to you too, kid."

"I'll apologize to Jeremy." And I will, but that doesn't mean I'll keep hanging out with him. I'm too humiliated for that.

"Great. You can do it in about thirty minutes."

"Huh?" Then I remember what day it is. "Oh. It's Friday, isn't it?"

"Poker night," Grandad confirms with a nod. "I'll see you there."

I'M so nervous I can't think straight. I don't think things would be this hard if I didn't have a huge crush on Jeremy. If he was just some guy, some random acquaintance, I wouldn't be so scared to see him. I probably wouldn't have run away when he saw the video. But he's not just a random guy. He's kind and gorgeous and has an interesting view of the world. He's someone I like hanging out with. He's not at all like Lane. And I know that I'll never get to be friends with him, not really. And I'll certainly never be anything more than friends. We live across the country from each other. It'll never happen.

Still, crushes are powerful things. My crush on Jeremy makes my hands sweat and my heart race while I sit on the patio of Grandad's house, watching all of his friends show up for poker night. Jan arrives with another container of cookies. This time they're lemon cookies with crystalized sugar on top, and they're amazing.

"Hey girl," she says as she sits in the chair next to me. She smells like floral perfume. "You look tan. Did you finally get some sun?"

"A little," I say, reaching for another cookie.

"Good, good. Sun is good for you."

"Says the woman who wears a sunhat bigger than an umbrella," Grandad teases.

"I'm old," Jan says with a laugh. "I have to protect

my old skin so I don't get as many wrinkles. Young people should be in the sun every chance they get, though."

She winks at me, then turns her attention to my grandfather. Their playful banter eases some of the tension in my joints, but soon I remember why I'm tense in the first place. Jeremy isn't here.

It's fifteen minutes after their poker start time and he's not here. I don't think he's coming at all. The rest of the poker players just get started without him, but I can't take my eyes off the patio landing where the stairs are, wondering if he'll come walking up late, with some excuse as to why he wasn't on time. In all the weeks I've been here, he's always been on time.

Three hours go by, and two things are very clear.

Jan has the hugest crush on my Grandad.

And Jeremy isn't coming.

I am consumed with guilt. This is all my fault. I ignored Jeremy all week because of my own embarrassment and now he doesn't feel welcome to come hang out with his neighbors like he does every Friday, since long before I was ever here. He has been nothing but kind to me, and I ruined this day for him.

Is it possible to fall further down after you've already hit rock bottom?

TEN

It's after midnight by the time Grandad's friends go home. I help him clean up the poker chips and fold the poker table which goes in the outdoor shed after every poker night. I snap the lid on Jan's container of cookies, which are half-gone by now. Every Friday she brings some kind of baked good over, and during the week, Grandad washes the container and gives it back to her only for her to bring it back filled with more food when Friday rolls back around.

"I'm sorry he didn't show," Grandad says as he hoists the folded table off the floor and carries it to the stairs.

"Me too," I say. My eyes are dry from watching the stairs, and my muscles are tight from a whole week of stressing about life. At the beginning of summer, I wanted things to go back to normal. But now, I'm not sure what normal is anymore. My home life is weird now that I'm living in my stepsister's ivy league shadow and my dad doesn't trust me. I haven't fully forgiven my cousin for letting me take the fall like that, and she's the best friend I have. I'm single and the whole senior class has seen me humiliated online. There is no normal right now. Everything sucks.

I bring the cookies into the kitchen and then turn and stare out the large living room windows at the ocean that would be pitch black without the sparkle of the crescent moon overhead. I try to think about the last time I was happy. Genuinely, truly, happy.

The answer hits me hard, like a surfboard to the face during a wipeout.

The last time I was happy was with Jeremy.

"Grandad?" I call out. I find him in the kitchen stealing another cookie. He looks sheepish as he snaps the plastic lid back on the container. I grin, my previous thoughts overshadowed by what's in front of me. "You know Jan likes you, right?"

"Of course she likes me," he says, his mouth full of cookie. "Everyone likes me."

I roll my eyes. "You know what I mean. She *like* likes you."

"Oh," he says. "Yeah I had a feeling."

"Do you like her?"

He shrugs, but even his stoic, expressionless face can't hide his true feelings.

"You totally like her!" I say, pointing a finger at him. "You should ask her out, old man."

He snorts. "I don't know."

"We all deserve to be happy, Grandad."

"Wise words from someone who has been avoiding the guy who *like*, likes her."

"My situation is different. It doesn't matter if he likes me. I live too far away and it would only end up hurting us both in the end. But you and Jan live on the same street."

"You don't have to go back home," he says. "You're family, after all. This is your home, too."

"Wait…" I breathe as the reality of what I think he's saying settles over me. "You're saying I could move in here for good?"

"That's exactly what I'm saying. It's been fun having you here this summer. And as I understand it, things aren't going so well for you at home. You could make new friends. Start over. And best of all, you could make sure your father doesn't try to sell this house out from under me."

"You're serious?" I say, my jaw hitting the floor. "You'd let me live here?"

He nods. "I'd be honored."

I rush forward and hug him. "Thank you," I say over tears I hadn't realized were forming in my eyes. Sterling Beach is an amazing community. He's right. I could start over. I could finish school here and then go to college and get to keep living in this awesome beach house.

Grandad hugs me back and then pulls away,

holding me at arm's length. "I do have one condition though."

"Friday night poker?" I ask.

"Not quite. If you want to live here, you need to get my favorite poker buddy back. It's not the same without that spunky kid who loves life."

I nod even though I'm a little bit terrified of the task at hand. Jeremy might be so upset with me that he refuses to join poker night ever again. But I made this mess and I'm going to do my hardest to clean it up.

"I'm on it," I say as I practically skip back to my dad's old room. If I'm successful, it won't be my dad's old room anymore.

It'll be my room.

ELEVEN

Since it would be weird and rude to show up at Jeremy's house after midnight, I forced myself to go to bed last night and wait until the morning. Now that it's morning, I'm lying in bed staring at the ceiling, trying to get the courage to apologize to the boy who didn't do anything wrong. It makes me cringe to think about how I acted. He didn't deserve that at all. If he doesn't forgive me, I won't blame him one bit.

It's not his fault that his friends showed him a video. He's been nothing but kind to me and I treated him like crap. My stomach twists into anxious knots. I don't know if I can get back the friendship we had, or if I could ever get back that little something extra we had. But I have to try.

I can't possibly move in with Grandad full time if Jeremy is still mad at me. And moving in with Grandad feels like the best thing for me right now. I could have a new school, new friends, and a new life away from my horrible step mom and her equally horrible daughter, who both have my dad wrapped around their finger. This could work. This could be great.

I just need to suck it up and make things right.

I wait until eleven in the morning, because I feel that's early but not too early. It's summer time, so Jeremy could be sleeping in late. I fix my hair and put on some lip gloss and mascara but I try not to make it look like I'm trying too hard. I'm not exactly sure how someone is supposed to dress when they have to go apologize for being a total jerk.

With a deep breath, I walk outside and over to the neighboring house. I've never been over here before since Jeremy always came over to Grandad's. The soft yellow paint reminds me of the sunrise. My heart is in my throat as I knock softly on the front door. A few terrifying moments later, the door opens.

A woman in her forties gives me a welcoming smile. "Hello."

"Hi," I say, trying to smile back. She has the same dark blue eyes as Jeremy and I know without a doubt that she's his mom. The resemblance is too striking for her to be anyone else. I swallow. "My name is Hadley."

"Oh, Hadley!" She smiles wider until it reaches her eyes. "So nice to meet you! I've been telling Jeremy to bring you around."

"You've heard of me?" I blurt out before my brain

can tell my mouth to shut up. I'm too shocked to shut up though. *He told his mom about me?*

"Of course, of course," she says, giving me this knowing look that sends all the blood in my body straight to my cheeks. "He's not here right now, honey. You can probably find him on the beach."

"Okay." I'm just the slightest bit relieved that he's not home right now. I know I need to talk to him, but I'm so scared I feel like I might puke. "I'll go look for him."

"You should come over soon for dinner," she says, still smiling. I think it's safe to say Jeremy hasn't told her anything about me lately or she wouldn't be smiling.

"Thanks," I tell her. If all goes well with Jeremy today, maybe he'll want me to come over for dinner, too.

I venture down to the beach in front of Jeremy's house and look both directions. I don't immediately see him, but with the dozens of people out here, he could be hiding in plain sight. I decide to walk to the south. My heart jolts every time I see a tanned guy in board shorts, but after a dozen of these occurrences, I still haven't found him.

There are just a ton of hot, tanned guys on Sterling Beach. Too bad I'm only looking for one specific hot, tanned guy. And I really, really hope I haven't ruined things with him.

After an hour of walking, my feet are covered in

sand and my whole body feels coated in a layer of salty air. I still haven't found him. Then, it comes to me. So clearly and vividly that I can't believe I didn't try this spot earlier. When I needed to be alone, I had found that isolated part of the beach and had taken refuge in it.

I jog across the beach as quickly as the sand will let me, and make my way toward that large rock that provides a shady area to sit. My heart pounds as I approach it, knowing that if he's not here, I'll be out of places to look.

I see a trail of footprints leading right up to the other side of the rock. Slowly, I walk around it, and find Jeremy.

He's sitting with his back against the rock, his hands pressed into the sand next to him. His eyes look over at me, but his expression doesn't change. I don't know if he's surprised or angry to see me.

"Mind if I sit down?" My voice is weak, timid.

He shrugs.

"Is that a yes or a no?"

His eyes meet mine. "It's always a yes, Hadley."

I sink into the sand next to him. "I'm sorry."

He doesn't say anything, so I feel compelled to keep talking. "I'm sorry for running out of the pie shop that day. Sorry for ignoring you all week. Sorry you had to skip poker night because I'm such a crappy person."

A muscle in his jaw twitches. "You are not a crappy person."

"Yeah, I am." I take a deep breath. "I shouldn't have left you that day."

"Why did you?" he asks, his voice sad.

"I was mortified. Your friends were playing that freaking video..." My teeth clench together to stop myself from crying. "I was just too embarrassed. I didn't want you to see it. I didn't want you to ever find out about it."

"About the video..." he says slowly, hesitantly as his fingers trace circles in the sand. "Was that some kind of scripted thing?"

I shake my head. "It was real."

"Your boyfriend broke up with you on YouTube?"

A ball of dread and hurt fills my chest and all I can do is nod in reply. Jeremy's arm slides around my shoulders and he pulls me into a hug. "God, Hadley. I'm so sorry."

My breathing is ragged and I'm trying so very hard not to cry. "It's fine. It's over. It's all in the past."

"No one deserves to be treated like that."

I shrug again. "I don't want to talk about it anymore."

"Okay." He releases me from the hug. I desperately want to stay in his arms, but I still have things to say.

"I want you to come back to poker nights. Grandad misses you."

He nods. "I will. I felt awful for skipping the last one, but I figured you didn't want to see me."

"It's not you… I was just so embarrassed. I'm *still* embarrassed."

"Don't let some jerk's actions ruin your happiness," he says. His hand reaches up and touches my cheek. When our eyes meet, a jolt of electricity ripples through my body. He smiles softly. "You are way too good for that guy anyway."

I lean against him, letting my body wrap into his, my face pressing to his chest. He smells good, like summer and happiness, and I want to say here forever. "Thank you for saying that."

"Hey… Hadley?" he says after a few minutes.

"Yeah?" I say without looking up. Laying against his chest, with his arm around me while we stare out at the ocean is my official favorite place to be. I'm not going to look up and ruin it.

"How do you feel about long-distance relationships?"

Okay, maybe I *will* look up. My lips press into a thin line as I hold back a smile. "What do you mean?"

Jeremy—always so full of confidence and a happy attitude—suddenly looks bashful. "I just… you're going back home after summer and… well…" He scratches his neck.

I grin. "I hate long distance relationships."

His face falls. "Oh."

I talk quickly because I can't leave him in a state of sadness for too long. "But what if we weren't long distance?"

Jeremy's brows shoot up. "What are you talking about?"

"Grandad said I could move in with him. Like, for good."

"Are you serious?"

I bite my bottom lip and nod. "Yeah."

That beautiful, carefree grin of his is back. "No. Freaking. Way."

"Yes way."

He stands up, then takes my hands and pulls me up with him. The sun is shining and the sand is warm beneath our feet, and on the shore, the ocean is swooshing water onto the sand, providing the perfect backdrop for a moment like this.

"Hadley," Jeremy says, holding my hands tightly in his. "Will you be my girlfriend?"

This time, the feeling of tears stinging at my eyes is from happiness. The next time I talk to my cousin I will have to thank her for throwing the party that ruined my life and then somehow brought about the events that saved it.

I look at Jeremy and feel my whole body warm up. "Yes."

ABOUT THE AUTHOR

Amy Sparling is the bestselling author of books for teens and the teens at heart. She lives on the coast of Texas with her family, her spoiled rotten pets, and a huge pile of books. She graduated with a degree in English and has worked at a bookstore, coffee shop, and a fashion boutique. Her fashion skills aren't the best, but luckily she turned her love of coffee and books into a writing career that means she can work in her pajamas. Her favorite things are coffee, book boyfriends, and Netflix binges.

She's always loved reading books from R. L. Stine's Fear Street series, to The Baby Sitter's Club series by Ann, Martin, and of course, Twilight. She started writing her own books in 2010 and now publishes several books a year. Amy loves getting messages from her readers and responds to every single one! Connect with her on one of the links below.

www.AmySparling.com

facebook.com/authoramysparling

bookbub.com/profile/amy-sparling

goodreads.com/Amy_Sparling